SunLit

Published by
Sundance Publishing
P.O. Box 1326
234 Taylor Street
Littleton, MA 01460
800-343-8204
www.sundancepub.com

First published 1999 by
Edizioni EL
Via J. Ressel, 5
34147 San Dorligo della Valle (TS)
Italy

Exclusive North American Distribution: Sundance Publishing

ISBN 0-7608-6715-1

Printed in Canada

Daisy
and Tina

Silvia Vignale

sundance

A Haights Cross Communications Company

Daisy and Tina

are sisters, you see.

They are as close as

two sisters can be.

Daisy and Tina

Tina is tiny.

She's really quite small.

Daisy is bigger.

She's really quite tall.

Daisy and Tina

play dress-up each day.

Daisy wears Tina's

small hat when they play.

Tina wears Daisy's
big, heavy hat.
It's hard to stand up with
a hat as big as that.

Daisy can carry

a toy box that's big.

Tina can carry

just one little pig.

Tina pretends that
she is a queen.

Daisy counts blocks

from one to nineteen.

Daisy has lost

her ring, and she's sad.

But then Tina finds it,

and Daisy is glad!

Daisy picks apples
off the tall trees.
Then Tina picks all
of the berries she sees.

Tina plays a horn.

She makes up a song.

Daisy plays a cello

and hums right along.

When they go swimming,

Daisy can float.

But Tina must ride

in her small paper boat.

Daisy and Tina
will color together.
They find things to do
in all kinds of weather.

When it's time for dinner,

Daisy has a big plate.

Tina's plate is smaller.

See how much they ate?

And when they are sleepy,

they get into their beds.

They drift off to sleep

with dreams in their heads.

Tina and Daisy

are sisters, you see.

They are as close as

two sisters can be!

Fun Pages

Have some fun with these puzzlers!

Can you find these things?

- Daisy's ring

- Tina's pig

- an apple

- a pencil

- Tina's horn

Daisy has made a huge sandwich. Point to each thing that she put in it.

SunLit Library